Bridget "Biddy" Mason

▲▽▲▽▲▽▲▽▲▽▲▽▲▽

Mason

A Walking Sensation

DWe Williams and **Loretta Ford**

Illustrated by **Joyce Jackson**

© 2006 DWeLo Enterprises

Visit us on the web at dweloenterprises.com

Library of Congress Control Number: 2006934757

ISBN: 0-9786839-0-0

To Vincent, Danielle, David

—L.F.

To Jasmine, Jordan, John, Jamila, Shawn,
Pam
and Jimmy

—D.W.

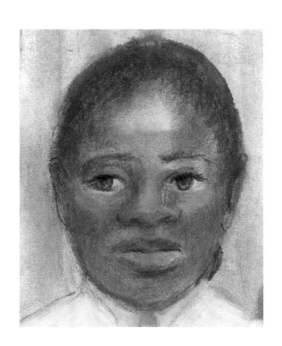

▲▽▲▽▲▽▲▽▲▽▲▽▲▽▲▽▲▽▲▽▲▽▲▽▲▽▲▽▲▽▲

About the "Peeker"

My mamma and daddy used to tell me that African
American people have always been a part of history.
Even though we were not always in history books, we
were a big part of history. We were great scientists
and mathematicians, teachers and preachers, doctors
and lawyers, entertainers and musicians, and inventors
and builders. When I "peek" back into history, I see
my ancestors there. I see them as early explorers. I
see them on the Trail of Tears. I see them in the
American Revolution and on board the Challenger. I
see my ancestors helping to build this great nation.
We were there, yes, we were there. We Were Always
There.

A special thanks to **RUDOLPH WORSLEY** for the
inspiration behind the "Peeker"

▲▽▲▽▲▽▲▽▲▽▲▽▲▽▲▽▲▽▲▽▲▽▲▽▲▽▲▽▲▽▲

When Bridget Mason was born on August 15, 1818, in Mississippi, her parents were so proud of their little biddy baby. Perhaps that's how she got her name "Biddy" Mason.

Biddy, Biddy, Oh Biddy, Biddy, Biddy Mason.

As a slave on Master Smith's plantation, young Biddy had to work hard just like the grown-ups. Sometimes she had to wash the clothes. Biddy worked hard for Master Smith for many years.

Biddy, Biddy, Oh Biddy, Biddy, Biddy Mason.

Years passed and Biddy grew up and had a family of her own. Biddy and her three girls continued to work on Master Smith's plantation.

One day Master Smith told Biddy that they were moving. Biddy and her children Ellen, Ann, and Harriett packed all of their belongings and prepared for the long trip.

Her trip started off in the state of Mississippi. She had a short stop over in Utah. She ended up in California.

Biddy, Biddy, Oh Biddy, Biddy, Biddy Mason.

Biddy had callouses and Biddy
had corns. Aching bunions were
not any fun for

**Biddy, Biddy,
Oh Biddy,
Biddy, Biddy Mason.**

What's a
Bunion?

Behind the last wagon she did walk, herding her sheep along the way.

Biddy, Biddy, Oh Biddy, Biddy, Biddy Mason.

With a stick in her hand and her girls by her side, her feet were getting tough just like rawhide.

Biddy, Biddy, Oh Biddy, Biddy, Biddy Mason.

Biddy had callouses and Biddy had corns.

Aching bunions were not any fun for

Biddy, Biddy, Oh Biddy, Biddy, Biddy Mason.

Some people told Biddy in California she was free. Master could not hold her as a slave any more.

Biddy, Biddy, Oh Biddy, Biddy, Biddy Mason.

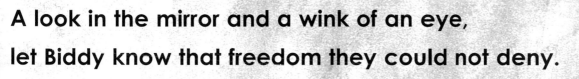

A look in the mirror and a wink of an eye,

let Biddy know that freedom they could not deny.

Biddy, Biddy, Oh Biddy, Biddy, Biddy Mason.

Biddy had callouses and Biddy had corns.

Aching bunions were not any fun for

Biddy, Biddy, Oh Biddy, Biddy, Biddy Mason.

Biddy went before Judge Benjamin Hayes in 1855, to ask for her freedom. On January 19, 1856, Judge Hayes granted freedom to Biddy, her three children, and her sister Hannah and her children too.

Biddy, Biddy, Oh Biddy, Biddy, Biddy Mason.

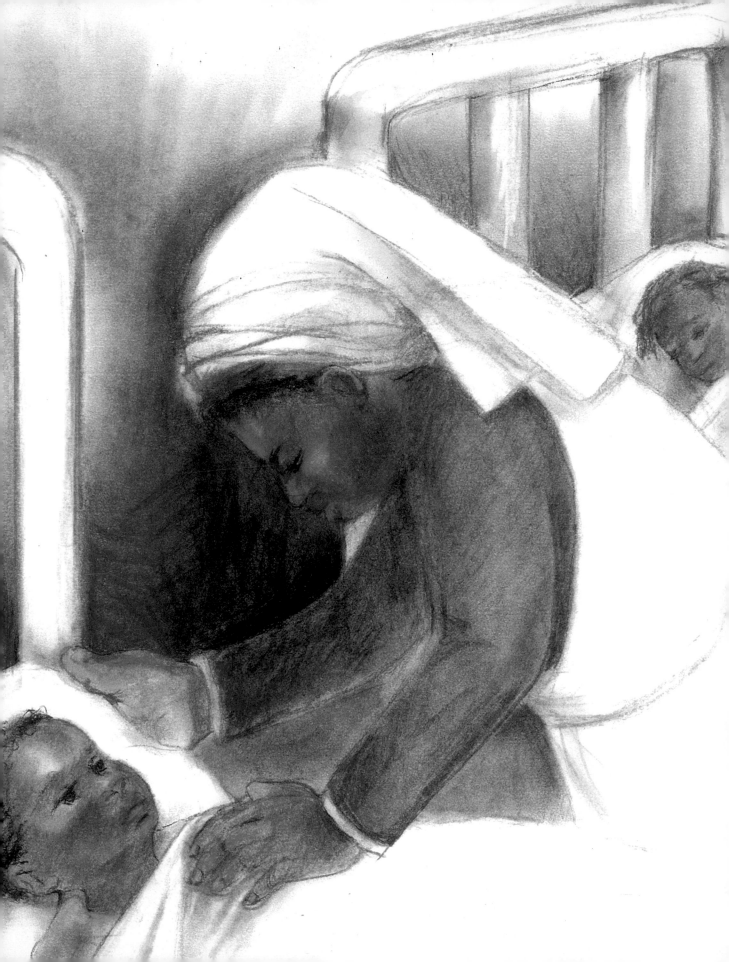

Biddy moved to Los Angeles with her children.

She was finally free. Biddy was offered a job as a nurse.

Biddy, Biddy, Oh Biddy, Biddy, Biddy Mason.

Biddy worked very hard and saved her money to buy land. She knew that owning land was important.

Biddy Mason was one of the first African American women to own land in Los Angeles, California.

Biddy, Biddy, Oh Biddy, Biddy, Biddy Mason.

Biddy Mason was a kind woman who enjoyed helping others. Whenever anyone came to town, they could always find a place to stay and a meal to eat at Biddy Mason's.

Biddy, Biddy, Oh Biddy, Biddy, Biddy Mason.

In 1872, Biddy Mason and her son-in-law founded and financed the Los Angeles branch of the First African Methodist Episcopal Church. This was the city's first African American church.

Biddy, Biddy, Oh Biddy, Biddy, Biddy Mason.

Biddy Mason was a generous woman. When Los Angeles flooded during the 1880's, Biddy paid for the food to feed many of the flood victims.

Biddy, Biddy, Oh Biddy, Biddy, Biddy Mason.

Over the years, Biddy continued to teach her family the value of saving money and buying land. Making wise money decisions helped her to save over three hundred thousand dollars.

Biddy Mason died on January 15, 1891, in Los Angeles, California. She left her vast fortune to her children and grandchildren.

Biddy Mason

Well, her trip started off in the state of Mississippi.
She had a short stop over in Utah.
More than seventeen hundred miles she walked.
She ended up in California.
Biddy, Biddy,
Oh Biddy, Biddy,
Biddy Mason.

Biddy had callouses and Biddy had corns,
Aching bunions were not any fun for
Biddy, Biddy,
Oh Biddy, Biddy,
Biddy Mason.

Behind the last wagon, she did walk,
Herding her sheep along the way.
Biddy, Biddy,
Oh Biddy, Biddy,
Biddy Mason.

With a stick in her hand and her girls by her side,
Her feet were getting tough just like rawhide.
Biddy, Biddy,
Oh Biddy, Biddy,
Biddy Mason.

Biddy had callouses and Biddy had corns,
Aching bunions were not any fun for
Biddy, Biddy,
Oh Biddy, Biddy,
Biddy Mason.

Some people told Biddy in California she was free.
Master couldn't hold her as a slave any more.
Biddy, Biddy
Oh Biddy, Biddy
Biddy Mason

But a look in the mirror, a wink of an eye,
Let Biddy know that freedom they couldn't deny.
Biddy, Biddy
Oh Biddy, Biddy
Biddy Mason

Biddy had callouses and Biddy had corns,
Aching bunions were not any fun for
Biddy, Biddy,
Oh Biddy, Biddy,
Biddy Mason.

DWe WILLIAMS is an accomplished storyteller, playwright, performer and educator. DWe, a graduate of North Carolina A&T State University and SIU Carbondale holds a Master's degree with a double major in Speech and Theater. DWe has seven children and resides in Oklahoma City, Oklahoma.

LORETTA FORD is an Early Childhood educator who has been in the classroom for more than 30 years. Loretta is a graduate of the District of Columbia Teachers College, and the University of the District of Columbia. She holds a Master 's degree in Early Childhood Education. Loretta is married and has two children. They reside in Cheverly, Maryland.

DWeLo PUBLICATIONS is a joint venture between DWe Williams and Loretta Ford. These two educators have combined their talents to create a series of children's books entitled "We Were Always There." This series focuses on the contributions and accomplishments of African American heroes. The first book in this series is Bridget "Biddy" Mason: A Walking Sensation.

JOYCE JACKSON is a retired Visual Arts teacher. She taught for more than 25 years in the Oklahoma City Public Schools. Ms. Jackson received her B.A. degree from Langston University. in Langston, Oklahoma. Joyce is an artist, teacher & Director of The Art Garden Studio, (a community based outreach project to encourage creative growth and expression). Her artwork is exciting and entertaining. This is her first children's book.

Coming Soon in the
WE WERE ALWAYS THERE series